ALLAN AHLBERG

Chicken, Chips and Peas

Illustrated by
ANDRÉ AMSTUTZ

VIKING • PUFFIN

VIKING/PUFFIN

Published by the Penguin Group: London, New York, Australia, Canada and New Zealand
Penguin Books Ltd, Registered Offices: Harmondsworth, Middlesex, England

First published by Viking 1999
1 3 5 7 9 10 8 6 4 2
Published in Puffin Books 1999
1 3 5 7 9 10 8 6 4 2

Printed in Hong Kong by Imago Publishing Ltd

A CIP catalogue record for this book is available from the British Library
ISBN 0–670–87991–6 Hardback
ISBN 0–140–56397–0 Paperback

Fast Fox wakes up.
He wants his supper –
chicken, chips and peas.

Mother Hen wakes up.
Her chickens want their supper –
corn, corn . . . and corn.

Slow Dog wakes up . . .
and goes to sleep again.

Fast Fox looks in his freezer.
Chips – yes!
Peas – yes!
But *no* chicken.

Mother Hen looks in her cupboard.
The chickens look too.
But *no* corn.

Slow Dog looks . . . nowhere.

The chickens go out
to find some corn.

Fast Fox goes out to find some chickens.

Mother Hen answers the phone.
Slow Dog . . . yawns.

The chickens look here and there.
They find a bat.
They find a ball.
They find a toy truck
with a teddy in it.

But *no* corn.

Fast Fox looks here and there.
He finds a beehive.
He finds a bee!

He finds a paddling pool
with a toy duck in it.
But *no* chickens.

Then . . .
the chickens find the corn
and Fast Fox finds . . .

T H

E M !

Fast Fox chases the chickens.

Mother Hen chases Fast Fox.

Slow Dog chases . . . nobody.

Fast Fox *catches* the chickens,
and Mother Hen too.
He puts them in his supper sack
and hurries home.

Then . . .
out of the starry sky
a big slow dog . . .

... falls on Fast Fox
and knocks him flat.

So the story ends.

The chickens get
corn for supper
and a bedtime story.

Slow Dog gets a pat on the head and a biscuit from Mother Hen.

Fast Fox gets a *lump* on the head,
a black eye
and a long walk home.

He gets his supper too.
Chips – yes!
Peas – yes!

But *no* chicken.

The End

FAST FOX, SLOW DOG

THE FAST FOX, SLOW DOG BOOKS

If you have enjoyed this story,
why not read another?
Try

Slow Dog Falling

In *Slow Dog Falling*,
Mother Hen is on the phone,
Slow Dog is all tied up,
Fast Fox is reading his cookbook,
and *chicken* is on the menu.

Oh no!
Those poor little chickens . . .

. . . who will save them?